Alfred Dixon Toovey

Eden and other poems

Alfred Dixon Toovey

Eden and other poems

ISBN/EAN: 9783337206345

Printed in Europe, USA, Canada, Australia, Japan

Cover: Foto ©Andreas Hilbeck / pixelio.de

More available books at **www.hansebooks.com**

AND OTHER POEMS.

BY

ALFRED DIXON TOOVEY.

LONDON:

LONGMAN, GREEN, LONGMAN, ROBERTS & GREEN.

1865.

LONDON:
SAVILL AND EDWARDS, PRINTERS, CHANDOS STREET,
COVENT GARDEN.

CONTENTS.

SCHOOL-BOY VERSES.

TO MY EARLIEST FRIEND

MY MOTHER,

I Affectionately Inscribe

THIS VOLUME.

ALFRED DIXON TOOVEY.

PREFACE.

As the preface to a book, like the bill of fare of a dinner, should raise no expectations it is unable to fulfil, I shall content myself with a very brief exordium. Of the poems in this volume the greater part are now published for the first time—some, however, were published in the days of my boyhood. I have two reasons for re-publishing the latter. First, they have been several years out of print; and, next, they won for me a testimonial, which I regard as one of my highest achievements. Of " Modern Life," Mr. Samuel Rogers, the gifted author of the " Pleasures of Memory," wrote thus:—" I need not say with what interest, with what pleasure I have read it, or how highly I shall value it as long as I live." This poem I have partly re-written, and, I hope, improved; but its structure remains the same. Of my more recent poems I will only say, that I trust the quality is not inferior. Without further preface, I leave this volume to my critics.

St. Albans, December, 1864.

EDEN.

"These are thy glorious works, Parent of Good.

* * * * * *

But neither breath of morn when she ascends
With charm of earliest birds ; nor rising sun
On this delightful land ; nor herb, fruit, flower
Glistering with dew ; nor fragrance after showers ;
Nor grateful evening mild ; nor silent night
With this her solemn bird ; nor walk by moon,
Or glittering starlight without thee is sweet."

MILTON.

E D E N.

"LIGHT let there be :" and God's sunlight appeared

On the morn of creation from Chaos upreared :

There was darkness no more on the face of the deep,

And th' Eternal said, " Time ! thou shalt wake from

thy sleep !"

On the face of the waters their Maker approved,

Lo ! His spirit the life-giving essence that moved ;

And the firmament fair, and all glorious and bright,

In a moment was formed, and behold there was light.

The dry land called He earth, and He bid the grass grow,

And the herb yield its seed, and the crystal springs flow ;

And the tree bear its fruit, and the earth wear a smile,

No sorrow to darken, no tempter beguile.

And the Word spake again, and the day and the night

Were the work of His love, and the proof of His might;

And life's essence He breathed:—how wondrous the
    birth,

As living things moved on the face of God's earth !

Lo ! the sixth morn arose, and Creation so fair

Was yet but a void till His image was there;

The bright sun might shine, and the waters might flow,

And the herb yield its seed, and the sweet flowerets grow.

All the beasts of the field, all the fowls of the air,

All the creeping things—works of His love and His care;

Of the sea all the fishes—the stars, moon, and sun

Were proofs wondrous and mighty His work was undone.

So the sixth morn arose, and—" Let us make man !"

Was breathed—and accomplished th' Eternal's great plan;

In His image he came : the work fair in His sight,

More mighty, more wondrous than—" Let there be light !"

" And dominion o'er all on the earth, in the sea,

Where'er there is life all dominion to thee!"—

With sorrow and trouble and sin, too, unknown,

As spake the Creator—" Creation 's thine own."

How fair looked the earth, which no sin had deformed,

When eastward in Eden a garden was formed;

As 'mid fruits and 'mid flowers our forefather trod,

All radiant and fresh from the hand of his God.

To the earth bow the heads of the beasts of the field,

Man alone to his Maker free homage can yield;

In His image exultant he looks on high Heaven,

His Maker to praise for the gifts He has given.*

Yet fair though the Eden with beauties untold,

With crystal founts springing and jasper and gold;

* " Pronaque cum spectent animalia cætera terram,
    Os homini sublime dedit, cœlumque tueri
    Jussit, et erectos sidera tollere vultus."
                                    OVID, _Metam._ lib. I.

To Adam there came from the high Heavenly Throne
A voice—"'Tis not good that thou shouldst live
    alone!"

Creation's work finished : at His high behest,
Lo! the creature of " all that's created the best ;"
More fair grew the Eden—see, see at his side,
Clothed with beauty and love, his joy and his pride.

And thankful he turned, " My Eve, dearest, mine,
Joy and peace are around, and stars over us shine."
Yon fleecy clouds floating above them so fair,
Were the curtains to cover their bridal couch there.

Oh ! fair was the Eden, for sin was unknown,
And the Maker said, " Good, lo ! the work is mine
    own!"
But lost soon the Paradise—sorrow and shame
Made the Eden they loved but an Eden in name.

Not for voice weak as mine be the tale of their fall,

Of the sin and the shame which yet cover us all;

Of peace turned to conflict, of love turned to hate,

Of the angel's sword flaming at Paradise gate.

Of Paradise lost mighty Milton has sung,

How the grim walls of Hell with the horrid deed

    rung;

" Of man's disobedience," how great was the cost,

When an Eden so fair and so treasured was lost.

More lowly my song—though the time has gone by,

For no sorrow to touch us or grief dim the eye;

Though we of the Eden so loved are bereft,

In God's gifts and blessings an Eden is left.

Ay, thus it is, loved one, I look on yon star,

And I thank Him who made it thou art not afar;

To my soul with its sweet silver voice though it cries,

It thrills not my soul like the light of thine eyes.

Ay, thus it is, loved one, I think in the night
Of the fair golden glory of thy beauty's light;
And I pray that old Time may touch lightly thy brow,
And the Heaven of thy smile may be ever as now.

There may, perchance, be in those bright worlds above
Countless myriads who live in peace, joy, and love;
With music seraphic attuned to their ears,
And cadences sweet in those mystical spheres.

There are flowers growing wanton that seek to be prest,
And murmuring waters to lull them to rest,
God's sunlight is pouring with soft golden showers,
To leave kisses sweet on the grass and the flowers.

There birds, too, are singing with notes sweet and clear,
"Lo! the springtime of life and its haven is here;
Here is manna for food, and when thou wouldst sip,
Here is nectar divine ne'er to fail from thy lip."

With mighty Hosannas the distant sphere rings,

And the seraphs are bright with the gold on their wings;

" Hosanna, Hosanna, all glory to God !"

Ay, bright as the Eden where Adam first trod.

" Hosanna, Hosanna !" triumphant the song

Which bursts uncontrolled from the worshipping throng;

" Hosanna, Hosanna !"   Oh, noblest of themes,

To fill our glad voices, and wake all our dreams.

Though Eden the lost ne'er the fallen shall see,

I only ask, loved one, an Eden with thee;

Ne'er a sorrow, a trouble, a tear, or a sigh,

But brightness and gladness for aye and for aye.

A NIGHT REVERIE NEAR ST. ALBAN'S ABBEY.

Heaven's lamps are shedding o'er these sacred walls
Their sweet and holy light, and lo! the moon,
More anxious than those clustering myriads,
Stoops forward from the sky and not to curse me:
I know these speak of peace, I know they tell
Of worlds where love and joy can never die,
I know they point to a far distant home,
I know they'd light us to that place of rest,
Yet while their silver voices speak, I feel
'Tis not for me, no, no, 'tis not for me;
My hand too feeble ne'er can clutch the bliss,
I know, indeed, that ye are beautiful,

And I have learnt to love ye, yet to me

There was one smile far dearer than thy light:

Ye starry hosts, though all of ye should join

In one triumphant anthem to your God,

Ye would not thrill me like her lightest touch.

She speaks again ; yes, once again mine ears

Drink in the heavenly music of her voice;

Oh ! let me crush deep, deep within my brain

The maddening melody of those dear tones.

Soft, soft, I dream, why do ye mock me, stars?

The clouds are gathering thick, no light is there—

I've lost thee in the mist.   O God, O God !

The night is dark, and one by one the stars

Have gone to rest close curtained by the clouds;

This chilling wind perchance is music there,

And lulls them to their sleep—would I could rest

Above the darkness with such calm content—

How low old turret frowns upon me now,

Solemn and dark as are these graves around,

Yet trumpet-tongued with warnings of the past.

A DREAM.

My soul is full
Of thoughts that scarce can shape themselves to song :
Around me are thy glorious works, O God!
Above me in unclouded glory shine the stars,
And all my thoughts pass back to that sweet eve,
When first I felt their power and loveliness.
Once more I wander on the lonely shore
Where first my soul was conscious that it loved ;
How after sorrow, trouble, pain, and toil,
Comes back again that day-dream of my life.—
My beautiful, oh! would that thou couldst hear
How cries my soul to Him who made these works,

That He will scatter flowers along thy path,

And at the end will lift thee up to Heaven.

'Twas fit beside the spirit-groaning sea,

My soul first learnt a worship deep as this.

Let me recall the time—seven summers back,

" And both were young, and one was beautiful;"

Time had just brought the dawn of womanhood;

Sweet sung the birds, and brightly shone the stars,

The jubilee of Nature and our hearts.

The Ocean spoke of love, the whispering winds

Seemed but to sing one low sweet song of love;

And then I loved thee, but my heart too full

Refused to grant my lips their utterance;

And so the time passed on, and Duty stood

With sword unsheathed before me in my path.

Four years had passed, and once again we stood

On that lone shore—the stars were still as bright,

The earth as fresh and green, the sea as fair,

As radiant with his image as when first

We wandered in that spring-time of our life;

And she had grown more passing beautiful.

The listening winds were hushed to hear the tale

Of love, but not, alas! of happiness.

She listened while I told of plighted troth

Ere first I saw her, how I kept my word.

And then my heart gushed forth, I told her how

My life became one fevered dream of her,

How every form of beauty to mine eyes

Her semblance wore, and how still more I grew

To love all Nature's works through loving her:

The bright deep sea, the face of Heaven itself,

I heard her voice, I saw but her in these—

How poetry became to me a passion,

And how, when hope was gone, my soul had grown

Up to a wild, wild worship such as this.

Three more years gone—here once again I stand

Alone to ope the annals of the past:

Lo! Time has risen with his healing wings

And been her comforter—her life glides on

In one calm current—am I then forgot?

That may be well—I would not have her know,

The troubled days, the dreams distraught, the thoughts

That festering lie within the aching heart,

The aimless life—ambition all shrunk up,

The cankering worm that eats into the soul

To leave alone that burning thought behind,

" Ye meet no more till comes the judgment day."

Not all forgotten yet—it cannot be

That when within that parting gift she reads

Of Him who " bindeth up the broken heart,"

No supplication e'er ascends to Heaven

That He may shed that holy influence here.

And in the calm clear eve when those bright stars

We sometimes watched together, which of old

Did teach the shepherds where the Saviour lay;

When shine these lights, she then perchance may think

Of one who had been better for her love—

Of one whose mind—shattered like drifting sails

When came the heart wreck—had its haven found,

With that one star to guide him in his course.

Farewell, thou mighty sea, the days are past

When thou couldst comfort me—I hear the groans

Of myriads of the dead within thy womb.

Ye stars! your light is false, ye may be worlds,

With countless human hearts that ache like mine.

A PICTURE OF LIFE.

THE tide of time rolls back—once more I stand

Upon the threshold of my changeful life:

My childhood's friends are all before me now,

My mother's gentle kiss, my father's smile;

I con the pictured books that pleased me then,

I tread in fancy all those garden paths:

Oh! I was happy as the singing birds

That fluttered in that spring time of my life.

Youth grew to manhood—Summer came at last—

The sky was brighter—louder sang the birds,

All Nature held her glorious jubilee,

The roses bloomed, hailed by the morning sun,

C

Who left his dewy kisses on their lips;

The sunflower wakened to the golden light,

The diamonds lay strewn thick upon the grass;

The sea was murmuring one unceasing song,

Yet not to me monotonous—I mused—

" These waters are untroubled, for they are

The reflex of a God beneficent,

Who smiled upon them in creation's dawn;—

And then I thought how centuries rolled on,

And how the waves grew troubled as the souls

Of Pharaoh's hosts and others, girt with sin,

Lay waiting judgment in the mighty deep.

Time travelled still—the patriarch days were
        passed;

Redemption's summer came, and One arose

Who walked the waters, and said, ' Peace, be still !' "

Thus mused I in that happy summer time.

To me the sea was calm; I heard no roar

Of raging majesty; the dove of peace,

As o'er the waters, hovered round my heart.

What dreams of fame! What hopes of high
    renown!
What aspirations for a laurel wreath
Dawned yet a brighter morn! Beside the waves
Another step was heard—another voice,
More musical than all those birds of song,
A face more fair than was that summer morn,
And through her love-lit eyes I saw her heart,
In whose pure depths methought I sat enthroned.
What was the world to me, its griefs, its pains,
When in that temple was my soul enshrined?
Old Ocean's music was one song of love.
Heart-bound we listened, till the eve put on
Her dusky mantle, and the stars shone out.
The summer passed away. When autumn came,
That voice was heard no more. She did not die.
Some said I loved her not, as scoffers tell
Eve did not love the Eden that she lost.
Oh! how she turned, and almost dared to brave
The flaming sword to win back Paradise.

So spring and summer went, and now, alas!

Where'er I walk I tread on withered leaves

Whose jaundiced looks remind me of the end.

Stern Winter comes apace with rugged front,

Cheerless and dark and icebound as my soul.

TO * * * *

———◆———

WOULDST have me place thine image down in memory's
deepest cell,

Where the hopes and fears of childhood's days in mystic
concourse dwell?

Wouldst have me quite forget the time when life was in
its bloom?

Alas! thou'lt give no flowers more, save they shall deck
my tomb.

Wouldst have me walk the paths we trod, yet think of
thee no more?

Wouldst quench for aye that lamp of love that blest my
heart of yore?

Wouldst have me, as I gaze aloft, forget that every star

We pictured a bright home of love,—nor feel thou art

 afar ?

It cannot be, thou dost not wish that *all* should be forgot,

The tones that charmed, the touch that thrilled, should

 be remembered not;

That never in far distant years thine image should be

 there,

That scarcely may I breathe thy name, or whisper it in

 prayer.

Oh no, tho' memory should bring back remorse, or

 grief, or shame,

Tho' it should quench ambition's fire, or blight my

 hopes of fame,

Tho' life should wither, and youth's blood flow sluggish

 thro' my veins,

Tho' the heart be sick, the brain be seared, the body

 racked with pains;

I'd brave the ills the boldest dread, the sufferings that
   they fear,

If memory brought alone with these that music to mine
   ear;

If thus alone she pictured still the bliss that once was
   mine,

Or Fancy warmed my heart again with that sweet smile
   of thine.

Or fair and prosperous be the winds, or troubled be the
   wave,

The star that ever guided me, shall light me to the
   grave;

When time shall pass, and bursts the soul all glorious
   through the sod,

Love shall not fade, but purer grow, for *all* shall rest
   with God.

HEREAFTER.

—————◆—————

I.

WE know around the mouldering grave
  No earthly charm can cling;
We know that He who came to save
  Has taught the song to sing;
We know that in that Holy Place,
  All worship Him alone;
Hosannas rise from every race
  That bows before His Throne.

II.

Though fairer flowers than these we love
  Should strew the paths of Heaven,

Yet the Spirit when it soars above,

   May e'en from such be riven;

With fruits of gold round jasper founts,

   Though crystal streams may flow,

'Tis not for these the Spirit mounts—

   To God it longs to go.

III.

The soul will have no taint of earth—

   The dust is 'neath the sod—

Yet again the body shall have birth,

   And both be joined with God;

And if this be, oh! tell me not,

   Though pure from touch of sin,

That all we loved can be forgot,

   When the soul is left within.

IV.

Will it not enhance a mother's joy

   To meet her child above?

Or must the grave for aye destroy

These well-springs of our love?

Oh! shall we feel no rapture there

Within that world of bliss,

If one be granted to our prayer

Whom we have loved in this?

ON THE DEATH OF E. M.

I.

WEEP not, oh ! weep not—thy wailing should cease,

When the life thus was holy, the end thus was peace;

Weep not, oh ! weep not—for over her grave

Shout the angels triumphant, that Christ came to save.

II.

The grass will grow green again, flowers spring around,

Though the death-worms are doing their work 'neath

    the ground ;

Yet why should ye weep ?—e'en the body will rise,

Re-fashioned by grace for its home in the skies.

III.

Though the summer is past and the autumn comes on,

And life's freshness is faded, its glory is gone:

You may picture her home in the realms of the blest,

Where the wicked ne'er trouble, the weary ones rest.

IV.

Then weep not, oh! weep not—though rude be the shock,

Yet Faith was her rudder and Christ is the Rock;

Weep not, oh! weep not—for time quickly flies,

And you'll meet where our God "wipes the tears from

    all eyes."

ON THE SAME.

———◆———

THE leaves were fast falling,
  The winds wailed around ;
When angels were calling,
  And solemn the sound :
With hearts full of sorrow
  We thought of the past,
·Yet we knew the bright morrow
  For ever would last.

We looked in the morning,
  And, lo ! she was there ;
And then came Death's warning,
  To find her in prayer ;

Yet cease your wild weeping,

Breaks forth from the skies

A voice to her sleeping,

That bids her " Arise !"

STANZAS.

———◆———

Methought that I saw her beside his grave weeping,

   As death pointed back to that dream of her youth;

No grass yet has grown—Oh! can he be sleeping

   So soundly he hears not the tale of thy truth?

He is gone, ay, and many have learned to upbraid him,

   For just ere he died 'scaped a word from his tongue,

It revealed all his grief;—behold where they laid him,

   There all that he cherished the requiem sung.

While his bark through Eternity's ocean is gliding,

   Is the compass he steered by forgot by him now?

Is that star which was ever above him presiding,

    Bereft of its light by a holier vow?

Weep not by his grave—the heart laden with sorrow

    Oft desires, though in death, a still earlier rest;

Weep not by his grave—but pray that his morrow

    May dawn with the angels proclaiming him blest!

TO * * * *

———◆———

I.

I ASK not here to meet again,

    Yet if my heart speak true,

The love that must through time remain,

    Will find its heaven with you.

II.

How sweet to feel the flowers we love

    Perchance may blossom there;

As seraphs' lutes melodious tell

    The joys we pant to share.

III.

How sweet to think those mighty worlds
    That shine above us now,
May light us to that bridal couch,
    And seal that mystic vow.

IV.

By Babel's streams to sit and weep,
    To weep, alas! alone;
To pass that dreaded Jordan-death
    Ere thou canst be mine own.

V.

To wander through this dreary waste,
    To watch the breakers' foam,
To climb the rugged mountain's side,
    Yet ne'er to find a home.

VI.

To walk the haunts of men among

Where some in peace can dwell;

To welcome tears of blood—to feel

That feeling is a Hell.

VII.

To dream of peace, to wake for strife;

To dream of thee and Heaven;

To wake and know my soul weighed down

With this mass of earthly leaven.

VIII.

'Tis sad, in pain, with bitterness,

To sow the seeds of love;

Yet, oh! how glorious 'tis to feel

The Harvest is above.

IX.

Ere many years the grass will grow;
Then withered be the sod;
Yet what of this—if ne'er we meet
Till both are called by God?

X.

Yet hark! I hear an angel's voice,
Oh! can it be my prayer
Is heard, where love immortal reigns,
And shall I meet thee *there?*

C H A N G E.

———◆———

I.

Is the bloom on youth's cheek but a moment's delight,

And the fire in youth's eye but a flickering light?

Are the hopes of young hearts, and the joys of young

    days,

Like the early spring flower which ere summer decays?

II.

Is the friendship of time but the dream of an hour,

When a touch can awaken, a breath overpower?

Is renown a mere by-word, and love but a name,

And all things else changing, do hearts change the same?

III.

From Iceland to Indus, go, search every clime,

On rocks or in caverns, on mountains sublime—

Do earthquakes ne'er move them, or lightnings assail,

Or the wolves of the forest ne'er howl in the vale?

IV.

Go, sit near old Tiber, or seek out each spot,

Which tells of the Cæsars though now *they are not;*

Where Tully once thundered, and Virgil once sung,

Yet the stones which they trod on are now all their tongue.

V.

Go, cry in the deserts, shall Babylon rise,

Or Gomorrah still lift up her head to the skies?

Go, ask of old Ocean—encroaching on land—

If in ages to come man's proud bulwarks shall stand?

VI.

Or gaze on the heavens, and ask of the night

If all things shall change in which man takes delight?

There—meteors are flashing with revelling flame,

Thus all things are changing, and hearts change the same.

TO * * *

WHEN thou treadest the turf that shall cover my clay,

And thy thoughts to those days of our boyhood shall

    stray,

When our life's golden morning comes back to thy mind—

Will a falling tear tell there's a void left behind?

Thou'lt remember how soon the dark shadow came o'er,

And my bark drifted on to that desolate shore;

Thou wilt think of the time when e'en thou couldst not

    cheer,

And wilt feel it was Mercy that sat by the bier.

Oh! who would live on 'midst this sorrow and gloom,

Could he know all he cherished would weep by his tomb;

That the birds would be singing for aye o'er his head,

And the withered flowers bloom again over the dead?

THE DEATH OF JOHN THE BAPTIST.

DEEM ye the hand of God withdrawn,

When hearts are by affliction torn?

Think ye His power, His will, His love,

Directs not wheresoe'er we rove?

Does not He guide the planets' course?

Does not His power the whirlwind stay?

Yet insect's breath is from the source

Which animates the monarch's clay.

O deem not, then, that He has left

His servant in yon dark cold cell,

Nor think Him of all hope bereft

E'en there where malefactors dwell.

For much of hope, nay, joy, is given

To this "blest messenger" of Heaven.

Though clanking chains may wrack his form,

His thoughts, his hopes, are fixed above;

Malignant leer, nor hatred's storm

Can aught avail 'gainst Heaven's love.

No tears of anguish here are shed,

All he resigns to God who gave,

Whose voice alone can wake the dead,

Whose arm alone has power to save.

For twelve long months within these walls

Has he been waiting for his doom;

Imprisonment nor death appals,

He thinks of life beyond the tomb.

At morn he wakes to pray to Heaven,

That saints be strengthened, sins forgiven;

At eve he lays him down to rest,

To dream of Heaven, and thus be blest.

Sent to prepare the Saviour's way,

Recall the wandering sinner home;

Convert and teach them how to pray,

And how " flee from the wrath to come."

This was his mission : could he, then,

Sanction a vice with splendour decked,

Pass by the deeds of mighty men,

And to their persons have respect?

Near to the cell whose walls enclose

Him who had preached of sins forgiven,

The palace of the Tetrarch rose,

In stately splendour unto heaven.

O what a contrast !   View the state

Of one in prison, yet elate;

Then see the monarch on his throne,

Forgetful of the Eternal One.

Yet start not, reader; doth not know

That Herod's heart was far from gladness?

And oft a cloud would cross his brow,

Which told his pomp was mixed with sadness.

And oh! what heart, though drunk with sin,

Can stifle *quite* the voice within?

His heart, though hardened, lost to shame,

Was staggered at th' Almighty's name.

He tried to think that when his breath

Should leave him, all would end in death;

He tried to think the name of hell

Was nothing but a childish spell;

He tried to think there was no Heaven,

(Could sins like his be there forgiven?)

And thus to quench the Spirit would he cry,

"My life, though holy, still my soul would die."

Yet man may strive: he strives in vain

To think death brings nor joy nor pain;

With Herod always thus: he tried

To lull his conscience with his pride;

And lately might be seen the look

More oft—the look of shame or anguish,

Yet would he ere a question brook

In gloomy thought and silence languish.

He felt that added to his crimes

Was one too terrible for thought;

He felt it, aye, and oftentimes

Would listen while the Baptist taught.

Yet why no profit?   Do not seeds

On stony ground spring up as weeds?

John told him of the world to come,

The mansions of eternal light:

He taught him *there* would be his home,

That *there* among the myriads bright,

Who hymned round the Eternal Throne,

Did he repent he would be one.

He told him that his crimes would bring

Vengeance from th' Almighty King;

He heard, too, of the unquenched flame,

And of the worm that never dies,

That when th' avenging Angel came,

He'd writhe in fearful agonies.

Herod would then turn pale and tremble;

Though ofttimes he had dangers braved,

He braved not now, nor could dissemble—

" O tell me, can my soul be saved ?"—

" Renounce thy sins," the Baptist cried,

" Submit to God that heart of pride—

Fly to the Saviour—hear His word—

And pray for grace when you have heard.

He came from God, yet walks on earth—

Your Saviour He ; though human birth

So lowly makes your heart despise

The One in whom salvation lies.

Yet hear again : thy brother's wife

Renounce—it is thy God's command,

And wherefore hope eternal life

If thus you His decrees withstand ?"—

Ah no! this was his darling sin,
And could repentance *here* begin?
No, like an insect fluttering round a flame,
Awhile he hovers, yet his end the same.

Nor was this all: at harlot's will
The Baptist was in prison cast;
Though Herod's conscience smote him still,
Deadened the dread of Heaven's blast,
Stifled the warnings of the past.
And thus it is man's stubborn heart
Will not submit to heavenly power;
Yet will with better feelings part
For the mere baubles of an hour.

And twelve long months had made his soul
More subject to such base control.
Behold his guests around him placed,
His halls with youth and beauty graced.

Yet who is seated by his side,

In haughty beauty's conscious pride?

Her name, Herodias—O! 'tis known too well!—

Her tongue a fury, and her breast a hell.

But, hark! soft music steals upon the ear;

And see a youthful form with grace appear.

'Tis young Salomé, in the pride of birth,

Who seems while loving it to spurn the earth.

Lo! while she dances, all the wondering crowd

Would at her shrine their very souls have bowed.

Nor mute their rapture; for by every tongue

Were told her merits, and her praises sung.

And Herod gazed as one entranced,

Nor could he passion's looks control.

And still he gazed, and still she danced;

And often, sidelong as she glanced,

A madness seemed to seize his soul.

The dance is ended; Herod calls—

Now all is silence in the halls.

" Salomé, come, I pray thee, here,

E

By kindred and affection dear;

Come, let me thank thee—(why is this?

Is it madness mixed with bliss?)—

O come, my fair one; nay, come nearer,

For than thou shouldst be, thou art dearer.

Ask what thou wilt, though half my throne,

I'll grant it thee, and thee alone."

O! what a power has Beauty's smile?

And what witchery her tongue?

Yet, ah! how oft it does beguile

The heart from right, and lead to wrong.

Salomé to her mother hied,

"What shall I ask?" the maiden cried.

Awhile Herodias silent stood,

And sometime communed with her heart.

First thought was power, the next was blood.

"Demand his head!   Nay, do not start.

Dost thou not know?   Canst thou not guess?

One passion we can ne'er express!

Nay, maiden; Herod loves my smile,

With me he would his hours beguile.

Yet once a scorpion crossed my path,

And think you mine is childish wrath?

'Twas John the Baptist; see yon walls

Which now enclose him; soon these halls

Shall see that head before me placed,

His blood a relish to our feast."

'Twas thus th' inhuman woman said;

To Herod then the damsel sped.

" Say, wilt thou swear that what I ask

Shall prove mine is no fruitless task?"

" I swear to grant whate'er you wish,"

Herod with passion quick replied.

" I pray thee give me in a dish

John Baptist's head," the maiden cried.

Oh! had those palace doors been rent

By lightning's flash, or had heaven's thunder

Now smote upon his ears, and spent

Its fury, scarce had been more wonder

Than Herod felt while gazing on that form

With look serene, but with a soul of storm.

Herod was evil; but the thought

Of such a deed appalled e'en him.

That he should murder him who taught

His soul, and for a childish whim.

" Ask something else; I cannot give

A life, nor shall he cease to live.

Is not thy heart more framed for love?

Dost thou not wish for wealth or power?

Let then thy thoughts through pleasures rove;

Let fancy paint to thee love's bower,

Or aught you will but this alone,

Though it be half a monarch's throne."

" Your oath remember!" cried the maid.

" O would that it had ne'er been made!

Will nothing else but this content?

If not, I cannot death prevent."

There was a pause, but not of dread;

It was a fearful pause of woe,

Like mourners gazing on the dead,

While earth is piled on dust below.

It was a fearful moment; now no tongue

Was heard in halls which late with voices rung;

The song was ended, and the dance was o'er,

The gorgeous banquet could delight no more.

Yet, hark! there is a noise without the halls,

Now noise than silence more each heart appals;

"It is the Baptist's head!" such is the sound

Which strikes each ear, and chills all hearts

    around.

It is the Baptist's head—and see the gore

Sprinkle the entrance, and bestrew the floor;

Lo! there, where late was youth's elastic bound,

A martyr's blood empurpled all the ground.

Now turn we from this scene of gloom,

And view yon cell, where late was life:

See that has passed beyond the tomb,

Removed from sorrow, far from strife;

Yet now the cherished friends arrive,

To bear his body to the grave,

Who oft did from his tongue derive

That knowledge which alone can save.

And why lament?—Through the Redeemer's love

His soul has soared to those bright realms above;

There will he ever with the angels sing,

Praise, glory, honour to the Eternal King.

A SKETCH.

———

THE sky was clear—'twas on a summer's eve

When we together roved along the beach;

And who would not luxurious dwellings leave,

When Nature's beauties are within their reach?

For Nature will the noblest lesson teach.

We talked of present and of future bliss

With fervour which, unknown to most, to each

Of us well known; we fondly loved; and this

Gives calm to sorrow while it adds to calmness bliss.

And still we wandered on, and talked of joy

And happiness, known little here below;

Imagination dreams of no alloy

To pleasure's cup; yet oft 'tis mixed with woe.

We lingered yet; meantime the heavens show

Signs of gathering storms, and the wild wave's splash

Now warns us to depart; yet, ere we go,

We turn to view the forkèd lightning's flash

Upon the waves, as foaming on the shore they dash.

Oh ! how I loved, in former happy days,

To view the mighty wonders of the deep;

Was happier in the storm than in the rays

Of sunshine : yet, O fatal memory, sleep !

I hate nought, love nought now : my mind a heap

Of ruins, and my heart a wreck.   No love

Now meets return ; no eye is there to weep;

No voice to cheer ; no smiles to pleasure move—

There is no comfort left except the One above.

We homeward turned our steps; we knew no fear ;

Her hand was clasped in mine; her eyes were bent

On me—for I alone on earth was dear

To that fair form.   A prayer to Heaven she sent

That He who could the raging storm prevent,

Would save His people from its fury now.

Her face was bright yet calm, as though were lent

To it the brightness of a seraph's brow,

Mixed with the solemn calm of the monastic vow.

Heavens! do I live, and think upon that night?

Her mild grey eyes were raised with love to mine,

The gloom around was by her smile made bright,

Those moments made her love the more entwine

Around my heart: but yet the Power Divine

Decrees her death—one flash—she falls—she dies!

My life, my love, O God, is only thine;

Her kindred spirit in a moment flies;

And why mourn I that she is wafted to the skies?

MODERN LIFE.

"Oh! in thy truth secure, thy virtue bold,
Beware the poison in the cup of gold."

S. ROGERS.

MODERN LIFE.

PART I.

THE sage's theme, the poet's deathless song—

Man and his life in converse with the throng;

The soul's bright gleams—the passion and the strife,

The burning quenchless poetry of life;

Life's varied scene and hope's fond fitful ray,

And musing mortals dreaming life away.

Not far from London is a fertile spot,

Which in man's vast *improvements* seems forgot.

There may we see the verdant village green,

And there the glassy stream may still be seen;

The modest church with ivy covered round,

And time-worn records in the burial ground.

There may we listen to the bleating fold,

Trace the rude carving—" Traveller, behold !"

Ah ! gaze around, ye mourners, ye may learn

Truths high and pure as those on " storied urn."

    Hard by the church the pastor's dwelling
      stands ;

His house but poor, of small extent his lands;

Yet had the Vicar never wished for more;

He prayed to Heaven, and Heaven had bless'd
      his store.

Oft, when he viewed the dwellings of the great,

He felt more thankful for his humble state;

And when he entered in the lowly cot,

And saw there happiness was oft the lot,

He was content with every blessing given ;

And troubles only smoothed his path to Heaven.

And thus, for ever happy and content,

For two-score years his life had here been spent;

His precepts taught but what his actions showed,

And with a love of good his bosom glowed.

The vicar, Mordaunt, passed his life in peace;

Nor as his age crept on did joys decrease:

A tender wife soothed his declining years;

A happy family at his board appears.

O! 'tis a blessed sight to find the one

We loved in youth, and sought and wooed and won—

When youthful passion sets the blood in flame,

To find this one in age can love the same:

The passion gone, a holier feeling shows,

More like to that with which an angel glows.

And thus it is we greater joy receive

From Sol's pure rays at the approach of eve:

The mid-day dazzles; but the setting light

Is far more welcome to our bounded sight.

And love, indeed, is blessed if it last,

To soothe the present, whisper of the past;

Point to the future, and with hope serene

Catch some faint glory of the world unseen.

So with the Pastor's wife: in youth she loved,

And in her age its truthfulness had proved.

Thus, thankful, they their race on earth had run;

Their prayer in every state—"God's will be

    done!"

Blest with two sons, and with those earthly joys

Which age ne'er weakens and no time destroys.

Richard, the elder, had seen thirty years:

The stamp of manhood on his brow appears;

An open countenance, a candid smile,

A bearing frank, devoid of art or guile;

Fond of his books, to learning much inclined,

He little studied learning through mankind;

He ne'er unheeded passed the house of woe,

Glad if relief or pity he could show;

Yet did he long to pass his days in peace,

And where his life begun would have it cease,

Near to the village church he long had loved,

Or at a fire-side whence he seldom roved,

Without ambition, he shunn'd all excess,

Nor cared for wealth, nor pined he at distress.

Not few his talents and not mean his mind,

Yet to a narrow sphere their aim confined.

And thus he passed his life, as only those

Who ever have in view how soon 't will close,

And all the transient joys of time shall be

Forgotten in one vast eternity.

Edward, the younger, was of different kind:

With heart as tender, stubborn was his mind.

His face revealed the sternness of the soul,

The haughty spirit which ne'er brooked control;

F

And on his brow men tried to trace in vain

His thoughts, his motives; yet they looked again.

E'en in his childhood did his parents mark

What in his eyes seemed like to passion's spark.

And what had Edward's youth been but the glow

Of feelings stronger than his age dared show?

Yet, 'mid ambition and youth's fiery zeal,

The moistened eye would tell how he could feel;

And often he, with faltering tongue, would bless

The needy soul, and comfort his distress.

Lo! manhood came—two passions for his guide

Swayed like a boat with adverse wind and tide:

The one—ambition, cankering his soul;

A fonder passion next pervades the whole.

His heart though proud, he loved the paltry fame,

The point of envy and the hero's name;

He loved to hear the whisper of applause;

For this forgetful of th' Eternal Cause.

Thus with the man who leaves the fertile plain,

The towering summit of some mount to gain,

Aspiring thoughts will often blind his eyes,

His way is lost—he famishes and dies.*

The Vicar had a brother in his youth,

Who married—died—confided to the truth

And watchful care of such a generous heart,

The last sole relic of his dearer part;

And little Mary, ere she had been taught

The name of parent, to that roof was brought;

And learned to lisp the name of God in prayer;

And, while she knelt, believed her parents—there.

Years had flown by, and she had reached the time

When youthful bloom is mostly in its prime;

When the gay laughter and the joyous mirth

Are left for thoughts now only in their birth;

When time has mellowed with its softening light

The joyous feelings and the young delight.

* "Tanto major famæ sitis est quam
Virtutis."

JUVENAL, *Sat.* x.

At that pure age, when blushes o'er the cheek

Feelings more deep than childish joys bespeak;

The faltering accent and the half-checked sigh,

The step more timid, though 'tis scarce known why.

But seventeen summers had bloomed o'er her head,

And round her form their radiance had shed:—

Yet she was fair as those whose fabled love

Lost angels their bright blissful homes above;

Dear—as remembrance to the broken-hearted,

Whose love remains when from the loved one parted

Pure—as the drop which falls from Beauty's eye,

And claims the heart-felt tribute of a sigh;

Soft—as the memory of childhood's joy;

Bright—as those hopes which time can ne'er destroy.

It is not form, nor is it eyes nor face

That give to woman loveliness and grace;

'Tis not the colour of the skin or hair;

'Tis not that one is dark, the other fair—

It is the mind must "harmonize the whole,"

The face must be reflected from the soul:

Still shone that soul each varying aspect through,

Like bright stars mirrored in the waters blue.

Mary would scarcely to herself confess,

That of the brothers one she thought of less.

Richard had ever been a brother kind,

Nor to his virtues had her heart been blind;

But mark the reddening flush when Edward came,

The heart's pure glow, and not the blush of shame;

Perchance that hand which trembled in his own

Revealed to him he did not love alone.

Nor was it strange: for when an infant, she

Was always happy on her playmate's knee;

As grew their love and onward rolled their years,

Each shared the other's joys, each dried the other's tears.

Still all things change, for lo! this happy home

Is now a house of mourning and of gloom;

The joyous step, alas! a noiseless tread,

See, all are weeping round the Pastor's bed:

This may be death; in truth, that silent room

Seems in itself to antedate the tomb.

The Vicar is contented and resigned,

With dreams of glory flitting o'er his mind.

Bright are the thoughts, when from the field of fame

The ardent spirit comes with conqueror's name ;

Dear is that joy when, after years of strife,

We clasp our all of happiness in life.

This may be bliss; but yet the panting soul

Feels more—much more—when hastening to its goal;

The hope, the trust, the rapture, and the dread,

Ere Hades opes its portals for the dead—

Yet, hush! he speaks:—" I feel my strength decay,

And hour by hour I seem to waste away;

Soon, soon—nay, weep not—will my spirit flee,

And live—O where?—in immortality.

" But yet, before I go, my children dear,

To my soul hearken, and my words revere.

Yet first to you, who with a watchful care

Each sorrow soothed, and every ill would share:

When I am gone, and o'er my mortal part

The green sod flourishes, then nerve your heart;

Do not as they, who without hope may sorrow;

To-day we die, yet shall we rise to-morrow.

Richard, to you is given the path I long have

     trod;

O ne'er neglect to feed the flock of God.

I do not doubt you; for the path of sin

Your soul would harrow ere you walked therein.

But Edward, you too oft have longed to rove,

For what?—The might of intellect to prove.

O check, I pray you, this presumptuous thought;

Fly to the cross of Jesus—there be taught

The mind must be subservient to the soul;

Presumptuous man must bow to God's control.

" Mary, in you I long have joyed to see

A heart as constant as a spirit free;

And thy young soul uncloyed by earthly joys,

That fond illusion which the grave destroys.

Canst thou not tell, tho' joys to all are given,

Who most appreciates the gifts of heaven ?—

Is it the restless soul that pants for fame,

And tastes of misery with a hero's name ?

Perhaps, like the lark, up-rising to the sky,

Sudden he falls, though he had risen high.

Is it the sordid soul who loves his hoard,

Or he who lavishes at Pleasure's board ?

Ah, no ! but is not he supremely blest,

Whose heart is peace, whose passions are at rest ;

Who calmly glides along this path of strife,

And sinks to rest—to wake to light and life ?"

The Vicar paused ; he looked around, and now

There seem'd a sudden lightning o'er his brow ;*

* " How oft, when men are at the point of death,
  Have they been merry ? which their keepers call
  A *lightning* before death———"

SHAKSPEARE, *Romeo and Juliet.*

As though his spirit in that gleam proclaimed,

His was a " hope that maketh not ashamed."

'Twas like the sun, the only good to bless

Some trackless path of a wide wilderness,

Though all would else be cheerless, still that light

Dispels the gloom and makes the desert bright;

It seemed for earth too bright, too pure, too fair—

A glimpse of what the soul might after share.

Yet, what of this?—It came, and it is past.

Each heart-struck mourner felt that sigh his last.

And he was gone; and many a tearful eye

Wept that he left them for his kindred sky.

And he was gone; his soul was winged above,

To the bright realms of everlasting love.

I will not dwell upon that week of woe,

Which there, at least, had not been heartless show;

I will not pause upon those days of dread,

Which passed before the burial of the dead.

Yet now the morn appears, when every tongue

Is heard in whispers; now the church-bells rung,

Not merry peals, but like a solemn dirge,

With sound more doleful than the midnight surge;

For though the ocean roars, the billows roll,

The lightning flashes, thunder shakes the soul—

They do not chill us like that stillness, when

We to the grave consign our fellow-men.

Two months had passed: nor had they passed in
    vain;

For every heart lost somewhat of its pain.

Now could they enter in that darksome room,

And even there forget awhile the tomb;

There was the seat where he had late been placed,

And there "the study" he so oft had graced.

Lo! these were passed unheeded by: the talk

Not always of him in his favourite walk.

Yet deem them not ungrateful: for the mind

Ponders but little on that theme—mankind;

Nor was it strange that they should seek relief,

When others seek it from a lesser grief.

Now Spring unfolds her beauties to the sight,

And vernal glories give the sense delight:

Now do the fields more verdant looks assume,

And man and nature gladden with the bloom.

It was that hour when in the Western sky

The sun was setting with a reddening dye;

It was the hour when music, from the throats

Of birds mellifluous, glides in liquid notes;

When most is tempered the heart's stubborn steel,

And man, if ever, for mankind will feel.

Oh! after all the hardships of the day,

If passed in labour, not in proud array,

Is it not pleasant, at the hour of eve,

To smile with man, or e'en with man to grieve;

To hold sweet converse with our fellow kind,

While mutual sympathy expands the mind?

Ah, yes! and did these moments longer last,
In which we ponder o'er the day that's past,
Man might forego some one ambitious aim,
And hearts now cruel might their natures tame.

But yet these peaceful moments may be cloyed
By those we love not, and th' effect destroyed:
By Mordaunt's family not unfelt the gloom
That Stranger's presence cast around the room;
And all the joy they felt before was now
Chilled by the withering aspect of that brow.
A man he was of two-score years or more,
Yet coming times had cast their shades before;
He seemed as though, were that indeed his age,
His life had halted at each foregone stage;
But age will ne'er appal us—you might trace
Somewhat of evil lurking in that face:
Perchance that sneering lip, that downcast brow,
Told tales of deeds he had not dared avow.

Yet wherefore here ?   He seems not one to roam,

Though he may gladden to make sad a home.

" You then were Mordaunt's wife?" the stranger said;

The widow murmured " Yes," and bent her head.

Not Scandal's tongue, while thus her eyes o'erflow,

Could tax her with the " mockery of woe."

" I knew him," said Howard (such the Stranger's name);

" Long did he seek my wayward youth to tame.

For years I have not seen him ; and my time

Has since been spent in India's sultry clime;

And now, returned to this forgotten isle,

I find no welcome and I meet no smile.

Yet have I that which, though 'tis oft called dross,

Our virtues trumpet, and o'er crimes will gloss :

'Tis gold.—I started a successful scheme,

And when 'twas won it seemed an idle dream.

I ne'er was one to value woman's smile,

E'en though the sunny daughters of this isle;

Still less in Ind.   Yet did I long for one

Who, of my blood, could not a father shun;

On whom to lavish all my wealth and care;

And, could I pray, for whom should be my prayer.

And then I married, and a son up-grew:

With him came feelings I before ne'er knew.

The mother died; nor could we smooth her pillow,

For o'er her body rolled the mighty billow.

And then, of course, the sounds of discontent

Were heard around: each gave his feelings vent;

To some enough to sneer at, or deride,

While others—'Lo! the murderer of his bride.'

" Yet were these sounds soon hushed; and all again

Once more was peaceful; but then o'er my brain

There came a fearful darkness: reason fled;

When sense returned, I found my son was—dead.

I will not tell you of those days of gloom,

Nor how I walked at midnight round his tomb;

It was that fearful stubbornness of woe,

When the heart chokes, and tears will seldom flow;

'Tis a relief, though snapping the heart's strings,

When from the eyelids scalding sorrow springs.

I tried to pray: but then my heart became

Tortured e'en more at the Almighty's name.

Yet time brought some relief; and then I felt

I worshipped Mammon, though to God I knelt.

"I stayed not there: thus heart-struck and forlorn,

The victim both of flattery and scorn,

I left for England; to this place I came.

By yon church-font was first proclaimed my name;

There is that village-school where I was taught:

Yet, ah! how little good that teaching wrought.

My mind was early warped to sin; and now,

I fear, the mark of Cain is on my brow."

The stranger paused and cast his eyes around.

"And have you yet from this no respite found?"

Asked Edward Mordaunt. " In this lonely place

But little is there sorrow to efface."

" Not so," returned the other ; " for to live

Where man one sympathetic tear will give,

Perchance produces feelings which renown

Would never bring—absorbs what pleasure ne'er could

    drown.

And I have marked in this long tedious tale,

Your sympathy o'er your dislike prevail;

Look in yon maiden's eye : there stands a tear

Which tells me that my woes are pitied here."

" I well remember," said the Vicar's wife,

" The dauntless daring of your early life ;

And when your parents oft your freaks have seen

From the bow-window looking o'er the green,

The youthful games you seemed the first to win ;

A mischief talked of, you the first to sin ;

But they who saw those freaks did not suppose

Their agèd eyes without your aid would close;

Yet soon they drifted down the stream of time,

With you forgetful in another clime."

" 'Tis but too true !   Not then to me were dear

Their smiles of pleasure, and their voice to cheer.

Perhaps e'en now I could not love a home ;

But that I hate still more than this to roam.

I left this place against my parents' will :

Lost then the only safeguard against ill."

" There is a better safeguard e'en than they,"

Said Richard Mordaunt; " one which can ne'er decay.

A firm reliance on that higher Power

Is the sole safeguard o'er each passing hour."

The youthful Vicar kindly pressed his stay,

While Howard talked of leaving day by day.

It was not that they loved him ; but there seemed

A spell cast round him like that sometimes dreamed—

A nameless something, a charm undefined,

That mystic offspring of a mighty mind.

We do not love this nature; but it seems

To rule our thoughts by day, and haunts our dreams.

We cannot love them, and we do not hate;

Yet such are oft enwoven with our fate;

Though oft they stand superior to all,

Yet when they sin, like Lucifer's their fall.

In reading, riding, walking, passed each day,

And Howard's gloom seemed partly chased away;

But yet not all, for will not such conceal

Those maddening thoughts which o'er the brain will
    steal?

And he was one of those who seem most glad

When the heart droops, and most the soul is sad.

On the first morning, Howard sought the ground

Where he had pleasure in his boyhood found,

And little wonder all the village talk

Of "the dark stranger seen in yonder walk."

And each one wondered "whence he came and why?

His step so haughty, and so proud his eye."

One would dislike him; and another thought

That "one so stern some evil deed had wrought;"

Whilst others said, that "they remembered well

A face like his, but where they could not tell;"

And each had somewhat to remark of one

Whom all agreed it would be well to shun.

Next morn he walked again; and then 'twas said,

"He looked like one but mourning for the dead."

Sorrowful, 'tis true; but each one viewed

That "with a Christian's heart he was embued;

His garb was manly, and his look was kind,

A noble person and yet nobler mind."

And what had wrought this change, and why should
    they,

Who shunned so lately, follow him to-day?

The night before he of his wealth had given,

And this the passport to most else but Heaven;

And they who lately hated that stern brow,

Followed, flattered, seemed to love him *now*.

Some few there were who would not yet caress

E'en the *kind* comforter of their distress;

They felt his kindness, but they also knew

He might do this, and yet be evil too;

Some few reflected that the road to fame

Gold often purchased; that a hero's name

Too oft is reached but by the shining ore,

And when that fails his glory is no more.

A week had passed, and now uprose the sun,

And, lo! another Sabbath had begun;

And there at least it seemed to be a day

When e'en the wicked some respect display:

Yes; all was silent save th' inviting call

Which those church bells were issuing to all.

The rich and poor seemed anxious here to share

The same good lesson in the house of prayer;

There is the mean-clad peasant, there we view
The squire and household in their high-backed pew;
All, all unite to worship Him alone,
Round whom the glories of the Godhead shone.
And now the prayers were over, and the poor
Halted a moment at the chancel door;
Each received something from the stranger's store,
So each one loved him better than before.

Man loves the best from whom he most receives—
The benefactor gone, the suppliant grieves.
But what of they who give? Sometimes, indeed,
'Tis the fair harvest of well-cultured seed;
Yet men more oft have with each other vied
Largely to give to gratify their pride,
Nor cared our Dives though the beggar die,
Unless the Lazarus at *his* gate should lie.

And how had Edward Mordaunt passed these days;
His name forgotten in the stranger's praise?

How had he felt, whilst thus around was thrown

The gorgeous mantle cast by wealth alone?

Natures unlike will sometimes love to join,

As base alloy is mixed with purest coin;

But yet more oft we find that men will herd

With those who echo every thought and word.

There was, in Edward Mordaunt, not the same

Unfeeling heart; yet each aspired to fame.

To him unknown th' impiety of pride,

One day to comfort, and the next deride;

By him unknown, that dread, that maddening thrall,

Which overwhelms the sense and deadens all;

But yet he felt a sadness o'er him steal

Which his pride would not for his life reveal.

He ever loved to wander forth and muse,

And from creation draw sublimest truths;

He loved to wander by the gentle streams

And picture forms seen only in our dreams;

He loved to walk by moonlight o'er the green,

And muse on what he was, and what had been;

His was a nature which desired apart
To scan the deep recesses of the heart.

Nor was that heart corrupt—a misty veil
Obscured its brightness, but could not prevail;
And oft, as morning mists are driven away,
And fogs are banished by the " king of day,"
So would the better feelings of his heart
Dispel the mist, and make his pride depart.

Edward and Howard had far different ends,
Yet some few views in common made them friends;
Though neither loved the other, yet each felt
That some resemblance in their feelings dwelt;
Each shared the other's long protracted walk,
The way enlivened by familiar talk.
Though oft opinions clash, yet each one found
The other's reason tread upon *his* ground.

It was one eve when the sun's setting beams
Shone in bright sparkles on the murmuring streams,

And the sweet sounds which issued from yon vale
Revealed the music of the nightingale;
Edward and Howard had beguiled the hours,
Viewing the ruins of some ancient towers,
That in a neighbouring village might be seen,
Where once 'twas said was bound a captive queen,
Where often afterwards was kept in state
The monarch's darling, and the people's hate;
Yet few men cavill'd, and 'tis surely just
To spare all royal votaries of lust.

From morn till noon, from noon till close of day,
With conversation they beguiled the way;
Nor as they homeward turned felt less inclined
To know the workings of each other's mind.
" To this we all return;" and Mordaunt felt
A sinking soul as on the thought he dwelt.
" Those towers," said he, " which we have been to view,
We less had thought of had they been more new;

Oh, how we love the glory that is gone,

The mouldering ruin and the worn-out stone!

On these the mind will dwell, yet what are new

Please us as baubles and like them pass too.

Yet these once mighty monuments of art,

Their glory gone, their ruins will depart;

And all will be ere many years forgot;

With tempests moulder, and with time they rot.

What now of mighty Babylon is shown?

No ruins there—almost its place unknown;

Yet some will give their health, their time, to stand

On what they guess is Babylonish land.

And why is it that man can love to gaze

On mouldering relics of departed days;

And even there, where nought around is seen,

Can love to stand for what there may have been?

Is it that man can love to pause on what

All nature tells him is the common lot?

Is it that he may draw from this the thought

That he, though mighty now, will soon be nought?

His glory gone, his very being dead ;
His body rotting and his spirit fled.

" Do we for this love on such scenes to pause ?"
Asked Edward Mordaunt.

      " I know not the cause.
But why such thoughts as these; and wherefore draw
Such strong conclusions from but Nature's law ?
From dust we came; at least so it is said :
And dust we may be, mingling with the dead.
Man follows man, like forms in Banquo's glass ;
Still thus as shades we come—like visions pass.
Yet what of this?   While living we should live,
And care but little what to-morrow give.
We cannot alter; wherefore tax our brain ?
We know no pleasure is produced by pain."

" I oft have wondered much, that with a mind
Which pants for fame, you can have fame resigned.

Since with you, I have marked the sudden glow

Which tells your blood is used to quickly flow :

I oft have watched your keen inquiring soul,

And thought that little you could brook control.

You might have won perhaps a noble name,

And in the path of honour sought for fame ;

Forgive me, if my friendship has transgressed,

You know your motives and your actions best."

" Is it not best to check too strong desires ?"

" No ; 'tis but fuel added to the fires.

Though meek-eyed Pity hover o'er thy hearth

And Love and Friendship strew with flowers thy path,

Kept in seclusion, soon the day may come,

Satiety may make you loathe a home ;

But had you seen the world and known its cares,

Its petty evils and its deeper snares,

You soon had felt that little else could give

More joys than this ; for this you then might live.

But has this place for ever been your home,

And have you ne'er indulged a wish to roam?"

" My childhood," said Mordaunt, " at this place was

    passed,   .

And every comfort was around it cast.

I reached seventeen : then first I felt the shame

Of life unmindful of youth's idol—Fame.

Then first I wished through the wide world to rove,

To seek renown e'en though I banished love.

With much entreaty I obtained consent,

And left this place.   To Oxford's towers I went.

My brother went before me ; and he told

What I should feel and what I might behold ;

Yet he was patient, could forgive the sneer

Which taught my soul to hate—and rankles here."

" And what was that ?" asked Howard; " I have

    guessed

There was a somewhat you had not expressed."

"My father was too poor to send me there,

With aught save what was needful, and his prayer.

I entered college; but too soon I found

My poverty despised, and wealth renowned:

A *Servitor*, 'twas thought, no insult feels;

Time only probes the wound, it seldom heals.

I had been there a month; yet, ere that, knew

The source from whence renown at College grew:

'Twas station—interest—wealth—and these at once

Make him a marvel who were else a dunce;

Yet was I glad that, in the public *school*,

' My Lord' had answered questions like a fool.

The titter which was hard to be suppressed

When his young ' lordship' had too silly guessed;

Yet when he leaves this place and walks the streets.

His hand is grasped and every menial greets,

While with a *friend* parading through the town,

He boasts of wealth, and interest with the crown:

And few men guessed, as strutting he would pass,

That much-sought puppet was the college ass.

" It boots not to relate the insult now,

Nor tell what branded ' shame ' upon this brow;

Marked youth's smooth front with furrowed lines of
    care,

When fools may trace th' inglorious record there;

I will not pause to tell thee of the wrong,

My cause, alas! was weak, for wealth is strong—

'Twas quickly proved that I had first rebelled :

' My Lord ' was mildly cautioned—I expelled.

" I soon left Oxford : to my home I came;

My spirits broken, overwhelmed with shame.

My father kindly met me; but too sad

That smile—that look—which late had made me glad.

Ere long he died : again I pant for fame,

And hope to banish what men call my shame."

" Mordaunt, my hopes, once fevered as your own,

Have been allayed; but yet the world has shown

That quiet brings not ever with it peace,

Nor in the busy world do comforts cease.

Do college quarrels give a branded name ?

Ah ! would that I had known no greater shame !

Then wherefore waste your life in scenes like these,

Which, awhile pleasant, soon will fail to please ?

Your talents soon your wishes will attain ;

Climb but the steep, the pinnacle to gain.

Here have I found that love may grow with age,

That here no time blots friendship from life's page.

Think not I am ungrateful : dost not know

One goodly flower on evil stem may grow ?

'Tis in the rugged earth we find the mine ;

And costly diamonds 'neath the surface shine,

I am not evil *all ;* but will you come

And share another, if less tranquil home ?

I would not have you live in listless ease ;

And little else are cares—are joys like these.

In London man may study more mankind ;

And this the noblest study for the mind."

" Yet is this true," asked Edward; " and do not
Such pleasures ripen but what time would rot ?
Methought, a week ago, you wished to live
Where man one sympathetic tear would give?
You cared not for the place; but thought that here
Was peace and quiet "———

                         " True; it did appear
That I could live in peace, nor care to rove;
But novelty is still my only love.
I ever loved the waves' tumultuous roll—
God's thunder aye was music to my soul.
Nor would I live with sunbeams o'er me showered,
If no skies darkened and no tempests lowered.
Nay; I have roved too long to care for rest,
The turmoils of the world still suit me best.
I soon must leave; I do not wish to part,
For kindness will plant interest in the heart.
My wealth and power would place you in a sphere
Where talents shine : they are unnoticed here."

" I thank you," said Mordaunt; " but I will not be
Indebted to another, though 'tis thee;
I ne'er will be by others' bounty fed,
Flatter and fawn to earn my daily bread.
O no! I here will live and here may die,
And know no change except futurity."

" No change!—the universe itself is change—
And changing creatures God's creation range;
Yon shining worlds that in their orbits move—
And man, weak man, inconstant in his love—
The fragile bark still veering in her course,
And empires rocking with an earthquake force:
Think ye, then, Mordaunt, that your life will glide
With scarce a ripple by this valley's side?
It is not so; for in those placid streams,
Which look so silvery in the moonlight beams.
Cast but a pebble: see the circle spread—
Repose is gone—the glassy beauty fled.

And so with you—awhile in quiet here,

You dream no ill, no danger can be near:

In thy life's dream be one small pebble cast,

Wide grows the circle—lo! thy dream is past.

It is not quiet—it is not repose—

Which can ensure that so your life will close:

Yet, if it did, you, Mordaunt, are not one

For listless ease a life of cares to shun.

In London, honour, power, wealth, and fame,

Will soon succeed to what you miscall shame.

Yet think it not a debt: have I not here

Had your kind counsels and your voice to cheer?

Or, if you will not in my comforts share,

Your own promotion there shall be your care.

Yet see your home at hand: now ponder well;

To-morrow morn your resolution tell."

And what thought Mordaunt, when he sought his
      bed?

"Yes; here, at least, in peace I lay my head.

Yes, here, at least, my friends are by my side."

And then a tear dropt from that heart of pride;

And then each precept that his father taught,

Before his soul with warning voice was brought.

" Yet how," thought he, " blot out my dire disgrace;

If actions do not, time cannot efface ?

My gentle cousin Mary, who is dear

As is the life-blood which is throbbing here;

For you, for all, I'll seek the path of fame,

And future deeds shall quite efface my shame."

Another week has passed: it is the eve

Before the day that Mordaunt is to leave.

Each long-loved face seems now to him more dear,

That the dread day of parting is so near.

Each thing has being now to Edward's eyes,

For that his home, and there his Paradise.

And so it was: though our first parents trod

The garden planted by the hand of God;

Though every good by Nature there was given,

And Nature's gifts breathed incense back to Heaven:

For this they might regret the judgment passed,

That they from such an Eden should be cast.

But, oh! what more than anguish 'twas to think,

There flows the stream of which they used to drink,

There are the paths through which they once had roved,

And there the bower where they once had loved.

Association gave the charm to this,

Or even Eden had lost half its bliss.

By Edward every path was traversed o'er,

As though he never should behold it more;

His constant dog, who ne'er from him had roved,

He felt now more than ever that he loved.

The saddened smile man's misery revealing,

E'en when he thinks his anguish he's concealing:

That doubtful misery, that uncertain gloom,

Which from the youthful cheek will steal the bloom:

Unlike the rosy tint of health and gladness,

The smile is but the hectic flush of sadness.

Ah ! who can paint those speaking looks that tell

Man's grief at parting where he loves too well?

Yet when in stubborn hearts these feelings rise,

And the soul's gushing scarce o'erflows the eyes;

When the heart burns, but will not breathe a sigh,

And sorrow's drop is glistening in the eye,

Grief still will gnaw, though we its cause conceal :

Man oft feels most when least he seems to feel.

But soon was passed to them that eve of grief,

And quickly each in slumber sought relief;

Yet, ere they went, they felt that one so dear

Claimed the sad parting tribute of a tear.

Oh ! few can tell how dear to Edward's eye

Was Mary's look of love, and parting sigh—

The brother's caution, and the mother's care—

And then the breathings of united prayer.

The morn arrives—what anguish 'tis to part,

To break the chain that links each loving heart!

Bright shines the sun—to-morrow he will rise,

And Mordaunt hail him under other skies.

PART II.

Can man thy fame—thy power—thy deeds rehearse,

Thou mighty atom of the universe?

Thou speck in matter, judged by form alone,

Thou hadst not glorious amongst empires shone—

'Tis not thy form would make thy name revered,

Thy favour sued for, and thine anger feared;

For, of the universe small space thou art,

A petty sparkle, which scarce forms a part—

London, thou world-controlling city, when I gaze

On what thou art, and know thy former days;

When I reflect that in this spot there stood,

In native grandeur, a wild trackless wood;

When I remember, here the incense rose,

That Pagan gods might crush the Briton's foes,

That in those streets which we so oft have trod,

Men sacrificed to idols, not to God,

I wonder more that thou shouldst empires guide,

O'er distant lands thy senate should preside.

Thy name is known wherever man may roam,

And far-off climes our empire—this our home.

Great heaven has wrought this change : the mighty plan

Were too amazing for the mind of man ;

And golden showers has God vouchsafed to pour

On this once barren but now favoured shore.

Imperial London, hail ! thy very name

Inspires mankind with love of wealth and fame.

Majestic Thames ! glide prosperous as thou art,

And still may England boast of Europe's mart.

Mordaunt sat musing in a gorgeous room ;

Nor outward splendour could dispel his gloom :

He had been there a week ; and Howard still

Enhanced each pleasure, lessened every ill.

Through Howard's interest he obtained a place,

(The name alone was surety 'gainst disgrace):

Employment was but nominal; and he

Received his stipend while his time was free;

And what he guessed, with human foresight dim,

A busy world, was otherwise to him.

" Is this ambition's end?" asked Mordaunt—while

His unschooled features wore a saddened smile;

" Is it the only aim of life—to live,

And know not, care not, what to-morrow give?

Canst thou suppose it is my sole desire

To live like this, nor food for love or ire?"

" Come, then," said Howard, " let us seek some place

Where novelty will soon thy gloom efface:

In this, your care, your thoughts, you soon may drown,

Nor fear the sceptic's sneer, the bigot's frown.

Life may be viewed afar, as we may gaze

Through history's page on deeds of bygone days;

Or as the man who from a summit looks

On sportive fishes in the distant brooks:

The object dimly seen—he cannot view

Distinctly from that height their kind or hue.

Thus, Mordaunt, you have hitherto seen life:

Think not you know it while aloof from strife;

Look *into* man—partake each joy, each care:

Then learn his nature while you shun the snare.

You need not, Mordaunt, mixing with mankind,

Let the world's baseness enter in your mind;

You need not drink so deep of pleasure's well,

That copious draughts should better thoughts expel;

As that is poison if we drink too deep,

Which, if but tasted, lulls us into sleep."

" We differ here," said Mordaunt, " for I think

We should be better did we never drink:

If once we sip, we long to sip again,

And when once tasted, our resolves are vain:

The cup is emptied to the dregs—too late

We find each draught has hurried on our fate.

Oh no, I do not long to take my fill

Of joys like these, and then be restless still.

Perhaps, e'en worse—my hopes may then retire,

My heart be vacant, and my brain on fire;

The poisoned waters rushing on my soul,

Despair or madness would pervade the whole;

And then, oh then, 'twould be too late to tell

What dreadful weight pulled down my soul to hell."

" You speak too strongly here "—

" It may be so :

Yet I would not the evils of it know.

I do not fear the tasting pain and grief;

An active life to me would be relief:

Yet, while I travel in the busy world,

I would not be in Pleasure's vortex whirled.

Oh, would that heaven would grant unto my mind

The praise—the admiration of mankind !"

" This," returned Howard, " is a dream of youth :

Your fancy soon will sink to sober truth.

I grant you, Pleasure may be fickle—vain—

Yet still there is enjoyment with the pain;

But in Ambition there is nought to bless,

Oft aspirations bring alone distress;

The goal is seldom reached : or, if we win,

There's less of pleasure, may-be more of sin.

In this, our modern Babel, you will find

Ambition's food, and charms of every kind :

Here is the Scylla of Ambition's wile;

Here the Charybdis of a wanton's smile.

You, Mordaunt, may shun both : dost thou not know

That only cowards flee the threatened blow?

The hardy mariner unfurls the sail

In stormy seas, as in a prosperous gale :

The wind may whistle, yet where'er he roam,

He feels his little bark is still his home;

Nor spurns it, though the tempests sometimes sweep,

And mightier vessels sink into the deep.

You must not shun the world, because in life

Is folly, anguish, misery, and strife.

But come to-night, and let me show you more

Of this vast city than you've seen before;

You never need again these scenes re-view,

Lost is the charm when they're no longer new."

Thus hopes may flee, and souls be lost—for what?

Man's resolution wavers from "will not";

Although experience will sadly tell,

That man's first waver is the threshold of his hell.

Mordaunt consented—it were vain to trace

What vice, what folly reigned in every place;

How first they went to view life's mimic stage,

See what men call "the manners of the age."

The object were not bad, if we could view

The colours varied, yet distinct their hue:

The stage would then reform and teach the times,

And not, alas, be but a school for crimes.

And shall our Shakspere pass unnoticed here,

Whose name each true-born Briton must revere?

Schooled in the heart, each varied passion drew,

Man as he is, he placed before our view;

Great in *description*, but oh! greater still

In praising virtue and in censuring ill;

He draws the tear and makes the bosom heave,

Truly paints vice, and makes the vicious grieve;

The colours oft may be too bold; but then

He paints not angels, but he shows us men.

Some few there are who show this life within:

While Rowe's great genius draws the tear for sin,

Jonson may make us smile; and Otway's pen

Show us alone the baser side of men;

Yet even Otway's low licentious talk,

Though plaintive vice through Rowe's sad scenes may

    walk,

There is at least one palliative, though small,

There genius writes, though it were vicious all.

But what the stage in these "degenerate days"?

Vice meets no censure, Virtue gains no praise:

Though sometimes Genius writes, he writes in vain;

The audience nod—then sneer—then nod again.

The mountebank—the pantomime—the dance,

Show how the tastes of Englishmen advance:

Now nursery rhymers wear the honoured bays;

Men prate of Shakspere, yet they *damn* his plays;

Unlike their forefathers, men love the best

The ribald laughter, the licentious jest;

And they who fall asleep o'er Shakspere's page,

Talk most about "the manners of the age."

And what could Mordaunt learn in scenes like these?

Their teaching could not profit—did not please.

They left the theatre—I will not trace

Their midnight wanderings from place to place;

Nor need I tell how they the night prolong

By miscalled pleasure, by licentious song;

Nor will I paint the Syren's hell-fraught smile,

The touch that taints, the accents that beguile :

The night was passed in sin; the morning rose,

And then our wanderers first sought repose.

Now Mordaunt slumbered—do not call it *sleep :*

He felt a serpent round his body creep;

The beauteous folds might well attract his eyes.

He feels the danger near; his agonising cries

Tell that his slumber has been fearful strife :

The visionary serpent stung him into life.

And what his thoughts on waking?   Did that start

Bring no remorse—no anguish to his heart ?

" Ah yes," thought he, " thus pleasure will entwine

Around the heart, and thus 'tis wound round mine;

Its colours too attractive to the sight,

Awhile it gives the finite sense delight;

But soon it stings, and its envenomed breath

Not starting wakes us; for that sting is death."

While danger lasts, hearts will some sorrow feel;

With ills around, men for protection kneel.

'Tis thus we see the timid soul will cower,

When lightning flashes and dark tempests lower:

He prays for mercy while the dangers last;

Forgets the Saviour when the storm is past.

When Mordaunt rose, his terror was subdued,

And in the evening were those scenes renewed;

Passion had once on Reason's barrier trod;

Then what cared he how far removed from God?

Pleasure begets satiety, and now

Dejection sat on Edward Mordaunt's brow.

A month had passed since first these joys he wooed:

The charm was gone; excitement was renewed:

For pleasure, at the best, is but a toy

Which children one day prize, the next destroy.

Weeks had passed on—o'er Edward Mordaunt's soul

The billows of tumultuous pleasure roll;

That heart grown callous, and that eye more cold,

Men in that flushing cheek his gaiety behold.

Strange, that thus man will his damnation drink,

And in repeated guilt his soul will sink;

Strange, that he cannot check his course of sin,

But on he hurries if he once begin.

Yet 'tis too true: as he who on the verge

Of some o'erhanging peak will gaze upon the surge—

O let him not upon the summit pause,

Oppose his finite sense to Nature's laws:

His brain bewildered—senses lulled asleep—

He gazes—totters—and falls headlong in the deep.

Soon Mordaunt's letters had less frequent grown,

For there were feelings which he dared not own;

He spoke less of himself and of his views,

And of the path which he through life would choose.

His thoughts of home seemed almost cast aside;

His letters seldom, and their subjects wide.

His cousin Mary wondered why her name
Was scarcely mentioned when the letters came:
Had he forgot they had together roved,
And, she had almost thought, together loved?
Had he forgot that smile of love and youth,
That smile so fraught with innocence and truth?
He scarcely could forget: but yet the soul
Leaves thoughts like these; guilt will pervade the whole;
Her name was sunk in Dissipation's stream,
And Mordaunt's love seemed now a boyish dream.

There is one vice to which we cling the more,
When pleasure satiates and delights are o'er,
We hug it closely as an object dear,
Although it brings mistrust, distaste and fear.
It is that mad ambition we behold
In him who seeks to win another's gold;
Restless, if fortune should oppose his will,
Or, if they coincide, he's restless still.

Mordaunt, ere many weeks had passed, could tell

The exciting pleasures of a London " hell."

The habit soon was rooted in the core :—

Thus, as the murderer sees his victim's gore

Rising in Judgment, ages perhaps flown by,

The dreadful scene still present to his eye,

He cannot, by an effort of the will,

Drive blood away—*there is the victim still.*

So is enwoven with the gamester's heart

The mad excitement, till of self 'tis part :

'Tis in his thoughts wherever he may roam,

The dice his treasure, and the " hell " his home.

O that the conscience, when it warns in time,

And tells the fearful doom awaiting crime :

When first it whispers, " Seek the only path,"

Or, when it thunders, " Fear the God of wrath !"

O that its voice were heard, before the grave

Proclaims its warnings are too late to save !

Howard would view his friend, and oft reflect,

" Here is the noble bark which I have wrecked;

Unfit to buffet the fierce waves of strife,

Or shun the shoals of a voluptuous life.

And now, unmindful of the stormy breeze,

He still sails onwards on the dangerous seas;

And little thinks he, that he soon may be

Launched on the ocean of eternity."

Man may not perish by th' Almighty's blast,

Nor see God's terrors as in ages past :

Do lightnings dart t' arrest a single germ ?

Or falls the avalanche to crush the worm ?

It needs no thunder, no destroying shower,

No mighty earthquake, no unusual power

To punish man : let God withdraw His grace,

And the worst judgment—the heart's vacant place.

There is no cry, no agonising groan,

Which issues from the bosom's burning throne,

Fearful as this :—" *Now I am left alone !*"

Was then this aid withdrawn, that Mordaunt's mind
Seemed unto all through mad excitement blind?
That he should tread the path where sinners trod,
Revel in pleasure, and forget his God?
The Spirit will not always strive. Mankind
May quench the strivings of th' Eternal mind:
Too long immersed in sensual delight,
Had Mordaunt's vices quenched that heavenly light?
It might be so. Forgotten now the prayer
For that high guidance, that Almighty care:
And now his appetite for pleasure cloyed,
And heart, and brain, and life—a senseless void.

When man would level doctrine to his sense,
And trust to Reason for his faith's defence;
When he would dare to scan those hidden things,
And solve the mysteries of the " King of kings,"
No wonder that he falls. 'Tis not for man
To thread the mazes of th' Almighty's plan:

If revelation were to reason clear,

There were no need of aught but reason here;

But shall weak man dare question what is good,

Because it cannot *all* be understood?

What need of faith, if reason showed mankind

The wondrous mysteries of th' Eternal mind?

Pleasure brings first misgiving to the heart,

Men's reason soon will greater doubts impart.

Mordaunt reflected—" Why a future fate,

When pleasure's woven with our present state;

When they alike who sin and they who pray,

May each enjoy what soon will pass away?

If Heaven ordains that men shall perish—why

Are some exalted to that unknown sky?

Or why should not Jehovah's mighty will

Crush into atoms *all*, for *all* do ill?

What can man add to the Eternal fame?

Then is not praise from good and ill the same?

What can man take from such a Being's might,

Who sits enthroned on everlasting light?

What can He care, to whom archangels bow,

What men refuse to hear or what avow?

When mountains are removed at His nod,

Earth's entrails tremble at the will of God,

What can it matter, though with trembling awe,

Men wait His judgments or despise His law?

If man can add no glory, nor detract,

Why should He follow not the smoothest track?

If the Almighty wills mankind to save,

'Tis not because this precious boon we crave.

Salvation thus depends not upon man,

For all is settled in th' Eternal plan.

Then let me live, and be my only care

Or to shun madness or avoid despair."

And this is human intellect, and here

Men dare to question who should only fear.

And this is human reason, boasted worth,

The pride of men, and to the devils mirth.

And know ye not, that e'en your vital breath

Draws in the element of after-death?

That though your intellect to heaven aspire,

There's fearful judgment in air's hidden fire?

It wants alone the Eternal Monarch's voice

To make men wail at what they now rejoice.*

Bad will bring worse: 'tis thus we see in youth

The strong desire to falsify the truth;

'Tis the first step to crimes of deeper dye,

And manhood's vice may spring from boyhood's lie.

So with man's reason: he will doubt awhile

That God can visit any with his smile;

His attributes he questions, and his laws,

And then at last denies the " Great First Cause."

---

* It is indeed an awful reflection, that what is *now* essential
to our being contains that element which may be our *hereafter*—
" *the fire* which never shall be quenched."

Pleasure and bad associates had wrought

In Mordaunt's mind such sad misguided thought:

Not long before, and he with horror viewed

The path he now so eagerly pursued.

Radiant with hope and panting with desires,

Such as the love of good alone inspires:

Once youthful ardour beaming in his face;

Yet, ah! how soon had vanished every trace!

Now, like a willow, would he hang his head,

A drooping form, and in his spirit dead.

The love of home and of a parent's smile,

But little now would Mordaunt's thoughts beguile;

Or e'en that love which man to woman owes,

When friendship joins the stream where passion flows;

That dear affection, fitted to outlive

Each other joy this transient world can give.

Religion—that was numbered with the past,

Uprooted like a tree by Afric's blast;

No traces left of what was late so fair,

The verdure gone—all was a desert there.

'Tis strange that man can live, and dare to think

Danger removed, while verging on its brink;

Though Mordaunt's state filled Howard's soul with awe,

Because he openly denied God's law;

Yet Howard deemed, that he at least could share

The self-same dangers, yet escape the snare.

He deemed himself secure: no words deny,

Though works offend, the Ruler of the sky.

And oh, how many who, abashed, will shrink

From the word poison, of the cup will drink!

An atheist!—Why start we at the word?

Why sink our hearts within us when 'tis heard?

That man should dare his Maker to deny,

Despise the Almighty, and his God defy?

This fills mankind, and well it may, with dread,

And calls down vengeance on the guilty head.

But yet the man who shudders at the name,

With equal madness if with more of shame,

Will cavil in his heart: and that recess

Would be ere long a pathless wilderness.

His principles, his actions are the same,

Though he is awe-struck at the sceptic's name:

An atheist in his heart—yet knows not how

His heart denies his God, although his lips avow.

'Tis thus the sceptic's icy heart will sadden;

And thus his brain, excitement gone, will madden;

Thus, like the lightning's flash upon the oak,

'Tis stripped in fragments ere is seen the stroke.

Yet Mordaunt still would seek his thoughts to drown,

Conscience to stifle in the din of "town";

The gamester's vice his greatest pleasure here;

The love of God forgot—unknown the fear.

Lo! he who late had sought in earnest prayer

Th' eternal guidance and the heavenly care,

Forgot, nay more, denied the Almighty power;

His sole desire t' enjoy the present hour

Mark yon proud building; was it built for fame,

That thus it boasts an almost royal name?

Is it intended for that converse sweet,

That social feeling when acquaintance meet?

It stands alone, a monument of art :

Does it improve mankind, and teach the heart?

Nay, does it e'en refine the sense, and show

Manners, at least, from intercourse may grow?

Ah, no : it stands, that man may pass the night,

Glutting on sin with devil's appetite.

'Twas built for vice : and this its high renown,

To deaden sense, demoralise the town,

That there, ere sickness wake them from their dream,

Nobles may gamble, statesmen may blaspheme :

Yet could they turn where sin will thus enthrall,

See as of old the writing on the wall,

And, like Belshazzar, view their judgment near,

Where then their pleasure, and what then their fear ?*

---

* It is sufficient proof of the pernicious effects of these estab-
lishments, that the *noble* frequenters should be found not only to
defraud one another, but should also endeavour to cheat the

View yon old man who totters to his sin;

His time-cracked voice scarce heard amid the din !

Like to some pilot in his ship asleep,

While winds are howling, and loud yawns the deep.

Hark ! from those lips what execrations flow !

They lately prated of a nation's woe.

O stay a moment, legislator, pause :

Shall worm like you despise your Maker's laws?

Is judgment such as yours to rule the state ?

Or vice like yours to weave the web of fate ?

No wonder than, a mist comes o'er the mind,

That without virtue intellect is blind ;

That folly you should add to your neglect,

Endow the college while you spurn the sect.

Why not conclude what you so well begin ?

Punish *each* sinner, propagate *each* sin,

proprietors under a plea of which they should be the last to
avail themselves.   This is not, I trust, the general practice, but
it would be easy to point to a notorious instance.

Draw on your fellow to a flaming pit,

See fire consume him—then display thy wit ;

Laugh, sneer, deride, revile him, if you will ;

But mark—the deed is thine, and there is judgment still.

Can we then wonder, though a nation cry

And lift its voice aloud in agony ?

Though direful famine stalk throughout the land,

Or War intestine lift his blood-red hand ?

How can we wonder if our produce fail—

Evil beset us, misery assail ?

Though mothers clasp their infants to their breast,

And cry aloud for death to give them rest ?

Though Darkness cover with his pitchy pall,

Or Terror's firebrand strike the breasts of all ?

Mordaunt had often met, within that place,

The man who was the cause of his disgrace.

His college foe was passed unnoticed by ;

Nor each vouchsafed to question or reply.

But on this night, while Mammon held the trap,

Resentment fled, and Lucre filled the gap.

Mordaunt had largely won the night before;

And Treasures soften e'en a foeman's core.

They spoke, they played—dispute ere long grew hig

Mordaunt, in passion, gave my lord " the lie."

In rage they parted, Mordaunt sought his rest

With body wearied and with mind distrest.

Next morn a stranger called: 'twas quickly shown

Blood must be shed the insult to atone;

No time for thought, resentment might be o'er,

But now 'tis *honour*, though 'twas hate before.

Honour—in blood congealed to take a life,

Which had been murder in the heat of strife!

Honour—when its results we dare not tell!

Honour—to plunge a fellow's soul to Hell!

Honour—to stand and be a murderer's mark,

To hurl defiance e'en with life's last spark;

To dare that law which has for ages stood—

" He dies by man who sheds a brother's blood !"

Oh, in that moment when we all shall stand

Waiting the judgment of the Almighty hand,

Will, then, this *honour* palliate the crime,

And Heaven's high Monarch hear the plea of time ?

Stript of those robes which make it honour here,

Before that throne the murder will appear ;

Disrobed of ornament, the sin is *there ;*

The crime is Cain's ; why not his judgment share—

An outcast on the Earth ; and in the Heaven,

O God ! can crimes like these be there forgiven ?

It was the eve before the fatal morn,

And Mordaunt sat dejected and forlorn ;

Howard in vain tried to dispel the gloom—

All was the lifeless silence of the tomb.

Mordaunt, too proud to agitation show,

Although too conscious of th' impending blow,

He could not help reflecting that he late

Was looking forward to a nobler fate;

That he had hoped with noblest men to vie,

And little thought that he in shame might die.

He trusted in himself—how vain the hope

For man, unaided, with his sin to cope!

And now to Mordaunt's mind were brought before

Those peaceful scenes he thought to view no more;

Those looks of love, that welcome with a smile;

He heard those tales which often would beguile;

Then like to felons with their lives at stake,

Who dream of peace and then to horror wake,

From his fond reverie Edward Mordaunt started;

Still deeper anguish had those thoughts imparted.

The dream was changed—he saw each happy face

Robbed of those smiles which time could not efface;

He saw his weeping mother standing there,

And heard her sobs and listened to her prayer—

" O God, have mercy; look upon my son!"

She could not murmur, "May Thy will be done."

He saw his brother at the altar stand,

And Sinai's law he held within his hand ;

And though he heard, " Thou shalt not kill," with awe,

He asked not God to make him keep the law.

He saw the weeping form of Mary now,

A death-like pallor overspread her brow ;

He saw that form now robbed of all its bloom,

Wan and dejected, hastening to the tomb;

That eye which late had lighted up the whole,

Told with unearthly light of a departing soul.

He saw the roses from her cheeks were fled,

The hectic flush of fever overspread ;

He saw her on her bed of sickness lie;

He saw her daily droop, and fade, and die.

And did no gleam of a preserving power

Glance on his soul in that dejected hour ?

Were there no thoughts of that great God, who gave .

The life which He and He alone could save?

Could he who late would scoff at and deny,

Now supplicate the Ruler of the sky?

Ah no! the thought once rose within his breast,

"Is there a God?" but could the thought give rest?

The thought was madness: if there was a God,

That he denied Him and with sinners trod;

He dared not think to-morrow he might be

Waiting his sentence for Eternity.—

O Fashion, wherefore always mar the earth?

Is this a time for folly or for mirth?

Is it a time, when man prepares for death,

To worship thee e'en with his latest breath?

Is it a time, when man would strike the blow,

To be the votary of heartless show?

Yet see the opponents to each other bend,

That you might almost deem the foe the friend.

The world's hypocrisy will thus beguile,

And take a brother's life-blood with a smile.

O God, that thus two fellow-mortals stand,

And impious dare the vengeance of Thine hand !

That each should quench the warning voice within,

When each may hurry to Thy sight in sin !

A moment more, and one or both may be

Waiting—but not with hope—eternity.

The ground is measured, and the friends retire;

The signal given—they together *fire*—

O God ! both fall : yet hark that parting groan !

Another soul has sought the world unknown :

The unerring ball had reached the seat of life,

And in one moment ended all the strife.

Mordaunt was yet alive; but from his side

Was swiftly flowing the ensanguined tide.

Yet, oh ! how fearfully those eye-balls roll,

Convulsive gasps his agonized soul ;

Stricken he lies, and weltering in his gore ;

Lo ! he may pray for mercy now no more.

E'en for his sins there now may be no moan ;

His soul seems issuing in each agonizing groan.

Ambition gone, and even pleasure fled—

See Mordaunt senseless laid upon his bed ;

And scarcely did he deem that life was there,

As o'er him Howard bent and breathed a prayer.

(When man cannot dejection chase away,

Though prayerless else, he then will try to pray.)

And then reflection came ; and Howard thought

Upon the work of evil he had wrought :

That his persuasions had induced his friend

Those means to follow, of which this the end.

For the wide waters he had left the ark ;

Though *there* was light and all around was dark.

He left those joys which he could not replace,

And sought, but did not find, a resting-place :

He found no verdant spot, no hopeful shore,

Though to the ark of peace he did return no more.

'Tis sad to see a fellow-mortal lie,

Verging on nature's last extremity.

'Tis sad to listen to each pain-fraught tone ;

To hear each sigh, and witness every moan.

But, oh ! what more than sadness 'tis to know,

That we have hastened the grim tyrant's blow;

That we have blighted thus a tree so fair,

And for spring blossoms left a winter there,

Accelerated death, and brought with death despair !

So Howard thought, as thus he bent to gaze :

" To me unknown he had seen happier days;

In peace had lived, in peace had been his death,

Not as a murderer resigned his breath."

" O may he live !" was Howard's cry to heaven ;

" Or if he die, to me be death forgiven !"

He had not done the deed : but yet he felt

The cause of misery with him had dwelt;

Not from his hand was sent the deadly shaft,

Nor had he held the cup which he had quaffed :

But who prepared the bow, the arrow fixed;

And who the poison in the cup had mixed?

His conscience told him he had sown the seed;

And this the produce of his fatal deed;

Cowed was that soul which ne'er had known a fear,

And from the Stoic heart gushed forth the bitter tear.

Behold him watching, by that flickering light,

That dying form through the long gloomy night;

How did he gaze upon that face so pale,

Those starting eyes, which told so sad a tale?

How could he hear the sinner's dying cry,

And listen to the murderer's agony?

He seemed one moment chasing round the room

The victim who through him had met his doom.

Anon he was upon a dreadful steep,

And plunged his victim headlong in the deep;

And then he saw him clinging to a raft;

He saw him sink—and then the murderer laughed.

'Tis sad such visions should float o'er the brain,

The mind be wakened by the body's pain ;

That thus the past should as the present seem,

And all be life-like in delirium's dream.

There is a solitude more sad than grief,

When the mind's torpor will not seek relief,

More sad than evils which may wrack and tear,

Yet leave not such a chilling winter there ;

To sit alone and watch a much-loved friend,

In drear unconsciousness approach his end ;

To watch alone the one that we have loved,

Whom long, long years of trial nobly proved ;

See those loved eyes cast an unmeaning glare,

And looks of love changed for that vacant stare ;

See the soul sink unconscious in the grave,

And know that we have not the power to save ;

To commune with the dying, yet no word

Escape the lips, but choking sobs are heard :

'Tis then we feel both joy and grief have flown;
And oh! how sad like this to be alone!

Yet e'en in this most lonely speck of time
The heart has some relief unknown to crime,
Can view the dying, can behold the dead,
Watch the poor sufferer when the mind is fled;
And though he watches with a soul subdued,
And feels how sad, how drear this solitude,
Yet he for better things life's path has trod,
And in this hour can commune with his God:
'Tis then he feels, there is a comfort left,
Though of the transient joys of time bereft;
'Tis then he feels, though other charms are flown,
The heart is sad, yet is not *all* alone.

Howard knew not this solace: you might trace
The gloom which time might lighten, not efface.
He had not known that comfort which, in grief,
Will consolation bring, if not relief;

He had not known religion will bring peace

When all the glories of the world shall cease.

There lay the one he loved but to enslave:

He could not see him sinking in the grave.

Morn came at last, and, with it, Mordaunt's friends:

A weeping mother at his couch attends;

A brother there, and more than sister too,

Gaze upon Mordaunt; and how sad the view!

How wild that look! is madness in the brain?

Or is't the agony of maddening pain?

How fixed those eyes! will those convulsive throes

Wrack that wan form until its being close?

How pale those lips! will they ne'er move again?

Or unto death will they death-like remain?

Will nought escape them, save that fearful cry,

Until the body moulder and the spirit fly?

Where then was Howard? He was gone—yet where?

He could not in the desolation share.

He left: and none could tell where he had fled;

If yet alive or numbered with the dead.

He could not stay to see how grief had worn

Those sorrowing friends—Morn came: and he was gone.

Hush! that look changes: will he yet revive?

Hark to the murmur, that "he still may live."

He wakes to life: but, ah! how soon that breath

Falters its accents, and will end in death.

Oh what is it, with such appalling power,

Makes death so dreadful in this dying hour?

That he forgets the friends who weeping stand,

And shrinks so fearfully from death's cold hand?

Men doubt not long there is a Power above,

Though they despise the working of His love:

Let them but feel decay around them creep,

And death be near them—is then fear asleep?

Think you that they who cavil for an hour,

With danger round them, do not quake and cower?

Think you those spirits that have walked the earth,

To jest at heaven and make their God their mirth,

When death was near them, could they then dissemble?

Ah no: they then had faith enough to tremble.

Think you there was no anguish, though no prayer

Came from the dying lips of a Voltaire?

Though Gibbon doubted, and though Hume would sneer,

Was it *all* doubting when their death was near?

The sceptic Shelley, with the sickly form,

Had he no fears of the impending storm?

Though poor weak man may almost doubt awhile,

Yet, on his death-bed, do these thoughts beguile?

Conscience then thunders that there is a God,

That death alone waits the Almighty's nod.

And lo! no wonder Mordaunt shrinks from death,

When to the God denied he must resign his breath.

His prayers avail not for a respite now:

The hand of death is laid upon his brow.

With one wild cry he's in his Maker's sight,

There to be judged by Him who judges right;

And could we hear the eternal sentence there,

If heaven or hell the doom—the lesson still—PREPARE !

A SELECTION

FROM

THE AUTHOR'S

SCHOOLBOY VERSES.

AN IMITATION.

He who has gazed upon the dying,
Ere the last spark of life is fled,
The spirit ere the time of flying,
The living struggling with the dead,
Through sickness long, disease or pain,
Has racked the body or the brain,
The soul will oft light up the eye
With brightness ere the spirit fly.
The brilliant flush upon the cheek
Seems immortality to seek;
Too bright for life, too pure for earth,
It is a heaven in its birth.

The lovely glow which ends in death—

The palsied frame, the quivering limb—

The struggles of the parting breath—

The eye now bright, before so dim.

Yet like to this are all our joys below,

A moment's brightness to an age of woe.

And when these joys approach " woo their stay,"

Yet ere we grasp them they have flown away,

And are, like loveliness with parting breath,

More bright and treasured that they end in—death.

AN IMITATION.

THE BURIAL OF A NAVAL HERO.

THE moon was mirrored in the unfathomed sea,
    And the stars in the waters were dancing,
When the pride of England was silently
    On her march o'er the Ocean advancing.

And all was still, and the sky was clear,
    Presaging a calm on the morrow;
Yet each eye was dimmed with a bitter tear,
    And each heart was laden with sorrow.

Ah, fierce was the battle, and long was the fight,
  And with horror fraught is the story;
For the foeman charged in the dead of night,
  And our hero fell 'mid his glory.

Now far away from the clashing of arms,
  We buried our warrior in sadness;
Nor the taunts of our foemen increased our alarms,
  Or goaded us onward to madness.

But silent and sad in the pale moonlight,
  We laid him to rest 'neath the billow;
For the Ocean was lately our hero's delight,
  And lo! in its depths is his pillow.

Our task now is done and onward we sail,
  With our glory consigned to the Ocean;
And if stormy the winds or gentle the gale,
  Still we think of the dead with emotion.

AN IMITATION.

FAREWELL, farewell, ye once loved shores,

    Where happiness and love were mine;

The Ocean with dread fury roars,

    Thus wielded by the Power Divine:

But when this dreadful fury's spent

    The Ocean knows some calm delight;

If I could thus my anguish vent,

    I would not say, fair land, " Good night."

Alas! the tempest in my soul,

    No momentary calm can know;

Oh! would I could my heart control,

    And bid a gentler current flow.

Yet what is it this anguish gives,

　　And clouds the days that were so bright?

Satiety all else survives,

　　And makes me bid this land " Good night."

Oh, I have tasted Pleasure's cup,

　　And drained the goblet with my friends,

For such they were to dine or sup,

　　But with the feast the friendship ends.

And I have basked me in the smile

　　Of some now joyless at my flight,

They cannot now my time beguile,

　　And therefore wish I them " Good night."

Farewell, farewell, thou once dear land!

　　I would not leave thee could I love;

I'll try Sahara's burning sand,

　　The blast of the simoom I'll prove.

Perchance that Afric's scorching fires,

    Some hopes, some feeling may excite;

For now are gone all fond desires,

    Then, why not bid this land " Good night?"

SONG.

I.

I LOVED thee in thy days of power.

I loved thee in thy pride:

Think'st thou in sorrow's darkening hour

I'd cast my love aside?

I loved thee when the fevered breath

Of fame first flushed thy cheek.

One voice alone—the voice of death

Can prove my love is weak.

II.

The world grows cold, but woman's love

Is warmer when it chills:

That spark of feeling from above,

'Mid life's ten thousand ills:

Love cares not for the sunny hour

When all around is bright.

But most displays its radiant power.

Like glow-worms. in the night.

SONG.

———◆———

I.

Go, tell to fools your dreams of glory,

The lightning blasts the laurelled brow;

The highest peaks are chill and hoary;

I care not for such visions now.

The world awhile may gaze with wonder,

We may be courted by the crowd;—

Yet—list ye to the approaching thunder—

For this at glory's shrine ye bowed.

II.

Oh! tell me not of days of loving,

Or of nights with rapture blest;

Ah! once what joy I felt in roving,

If not beloved, at least caressed.

Yet now the heart is seared—forsaken—

Glory, love, and honour gone:

Would that Thine Hand my life had taken,

Ere Thou hadst left my soul forlorn.

SONG.

I.

This world is not so dreary,

There's many a flowery mead;

Green hillocks for the weary,

And manna for our need;

There are oceans wide of kindness

Around us every flow,

Tho' we see not in our blindness

The treasure caves below.

Then carp not at this beauteous earth,

Then rail not 'gainst thy brother,

But set them at their Maker's worth,

By loving one another.

II.

There's music in the roughest heart,

Could we but strike the chord;

For man retains, tho' but in part,

Some likeness of his Lord.

There's friendship left if love be lost;

No blast life's tree has riven;—

The ship sails on, tho' tempest tost,

Her beacon light in Heaven.

Oh ! carp not at this glorious earth,

Oh ! rail not 'gainst thy brother,

For both reflect their Maker's worth,

Then love ye one another.

FRAGMENTS FROM "TIME," A POEM.

———◆———

YE many twinkling stars that stud the sky

And deck with brightness yon blue canopy ;

Thou lesser orb, yet greater to our sight,

And all ye beauteous ministers of night,

Ye teach this lesson—"All shall fade away,"

As ye do now beneath the God of Day.

A few short hours, while we may smile or weep,

And ye again shall shine and Nature sleep—

Yet when man fades, his radiance is o'er ;

Unless renewed he lives, to fade no more.

    *   *   *   *   *

Oh ! what vast records both of pain and crime,

Of joys, and hopes, and fears, are wrapt in Time.

First in the cradle is the fretful child :

Then years of youthful hopes, and fancies wild,

When the heart burns and passions wildly flow,

And to God's offer pride gives answer "No;"

When each besetting sin around us lies—

While on ambition's wing we mount the skies—

Then fierce desires will hold the sovereign sway,

And with their whirlwind force sweep sense away;

Then, then we seek the friendship of a crowd,

And fame which passes like the summer's cloud.

Then, too forgetful that these joys soon die,

We stifle thoughts of immortality.

*   *   *   *   *

What art thou to Eternity, O Time?

One spot to an immeasurable clime!

One flickering ray, one fitful gleam of light,

To shining suns by day, or stars by night.

One drop of water to the unfathomed sea,

One chain unloosed to myriad captives free,

These, these are still a part, but what art thou,

Eternity?—A never ending now—

Age after age shall still unnoted fly,

And sinners endless supplicate—to die.

O God—the thought is terrible—how vast

That mighty space when part is never past—

Though million seasons o'er our heads shall roll,

Eternity still endless—as the soul.

* * * * *

Oh! blest, for ever to be blest are they,

Who for that endless morrow live to-day;

Who build no hopes upon the shifting sand

Which on the rock of adamant should stand.

Who leave not God for Mammon in their youth,

Nor make a jest and byword of the truth,

Who strive the dangerous shoals of life to shun,

Nor grasp at Heaven by deeds which they have done;

But, gazing on that Pilot who will steer

Their barks hereafter if He guide them here,

Shall still press onward for that hallowed shore,

And live in bliss when "Time" shall be no more.

THE END.

www.ingramcontent.com/pod-product-compliance
Lightning Source LLC
Chambersburg PA
CBHW031118020726
47495CB00007B/2246